FUNIMALS

For Mark Infield P.R.
For Karen C.F.

FUNIMALS

Written by Paul Rogers

Illustrated by Charles Fuge

AUTHOR ROGERS, P

TITLE FUNIMALS

RED FOX

What's this animal? Do you know?

A buffalump or a buffalo?

Flipping its wings and waddling along –
A penguin or a pingopong?

Scaly skin and a nasty smile –
A crocosnap or a crocodile?

Stretching its claws and swishing its tail—
A tiger or a stripingale?

A jungle bird that can learn to talk –
A parrot or a parrosquawk?

Holding paws in the icy air –
A roly pole or a polar bear?

An ugly face from the day it was born —
A rhino or a runcihorn?

Taking a ride on its mother's back –

A koala or a carryjack?

Born with a big warm coat to wear –
A groozle or a grizzly bear?

Sharp as a needle, each prickly spine –
A porcupuss or a porcupine?

Taller
than
all
the
others
by
—half—

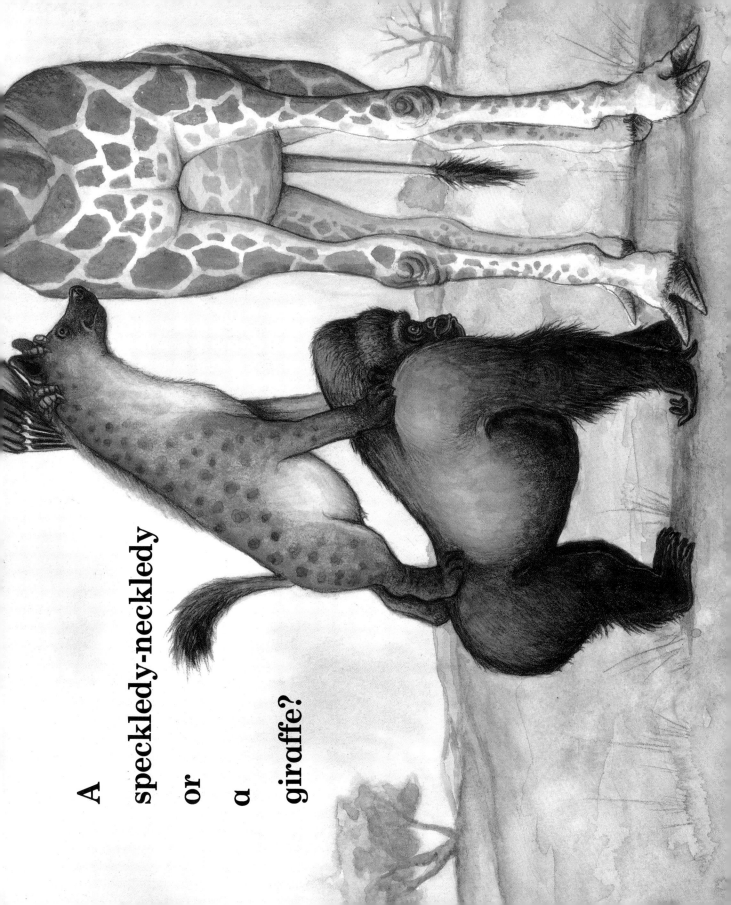

A
speckledy-neckledy
or
a
giraffe?

Big black eyes and ears to match –
A panda or a paddypatch?

A bit like you and a bit like me –
A chimpanzoo or a chimpanzee?

A Red Fox Book

Published by Random Century Children's Books
20 Vauxhall Bridge Road, London SW1V 2SA

A division of the Random Century Group
London Melbourne Sydney Auckland
Johannesburg and agencies throughout the world

First published by The Bodley Head Children's Books 1991

Red Fox edition 1992

Printed in Singapore